Mel Bay Presents

Daily Scale Exercises for Violin

by Herbert Chang

D1616705

2 3 4 5 6 7 8 9 0

Visit us on the Web at www.melbay.com — E-mail us at email@melbay.com

Contents

Preface

Mastering all 24 major and minor scales can significantly improve violinists' technique. However, through the years, not many people have tried to do so because it takes too much time and energy. Now, this book is designed to help people solve this problem.

In this book, I first classify all the fingerings of the single-stop scales into only a few basic patterns. When studying, students can learn these fingering patterns first and then use them to play all 24 scales easily. Then I re-organize the double-stop scales to make them simple, practical, and easy to learn.

With these improvements, the learning process for violin scales is much easier than before. Therefore, in using this book, most violinists should be able to master all 24 scales without an unacceptable cost in time and energy. For those who are not interested in studying all the scales, this book still can provide a simple and more practical method to help them better master violin scales with less cost in time and energy.

Bowings and Rhythms

Violin scales should be practiced with a variety of bowings and rhythms. More variation makes far better exercises. In this book, several bowings and rhythms are listed. When practicing, you may try other variations as well which can best serve your own needs.

BOWINGS AND RHYTHMS FOR SINGLE-STOP SCALES

BOWINGS AND RHYTHMS FOR ARPEGGIOS

* The variations below are designed for 7th Chords

BOWINGS AND RHYTHMS FOR DOUBLE-STOP SCALES

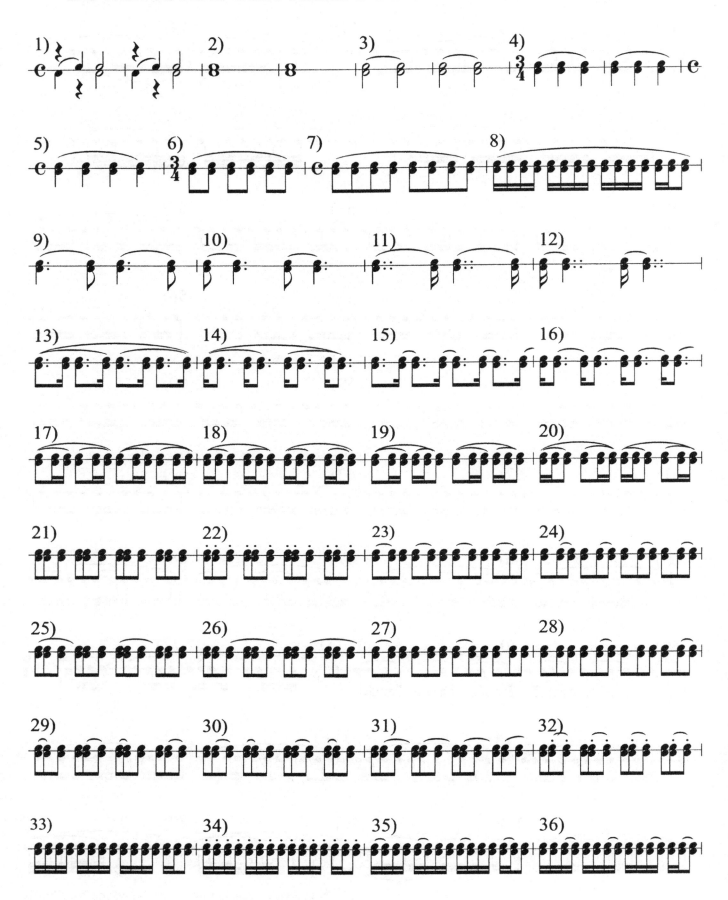

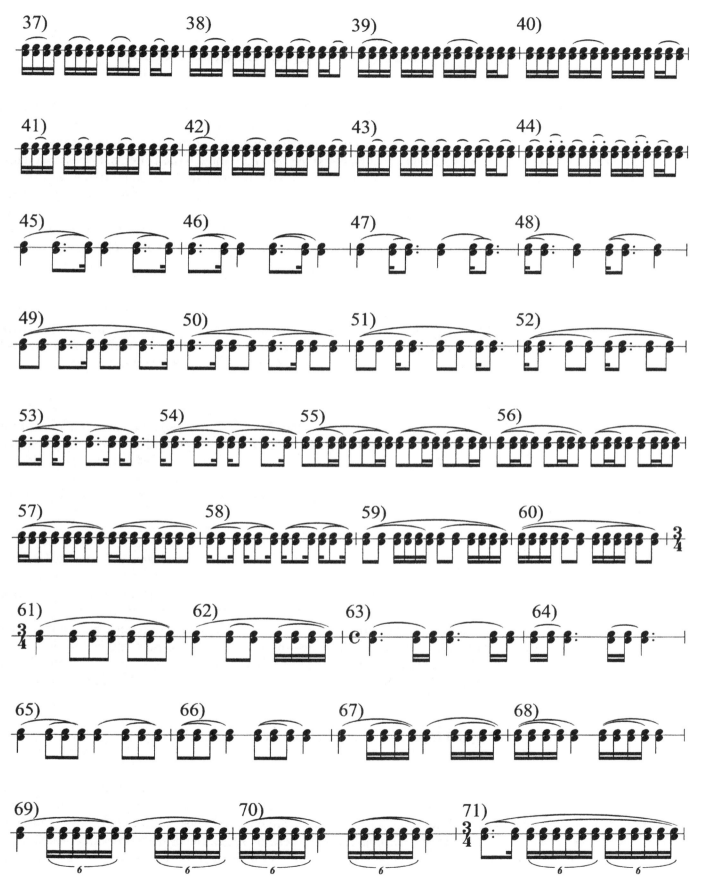

PART 1. DAILY SCALE EXERCISES

Fingering Patterns for Three-Octave Scales

"DAILY SCALE EXERCISES" is the main body of this book. There are 24 three-octave and double-stop scales in this part. And in the category of the three-octave scales, there are also four different exercises: scales, arpeggios, broken thirds, and chromatic scales. That's a lot of materials. However, except for the chromatic scales, all the fingerings of the other three exercises actually can be classified into only three basic patterns. (Please reference Fingering Table 1A.) The first pattern is the fingering that starts with the open string G. This type of fingering is only used to play the G major and G minor scales. The second pattern begins with the first finger. It is used to play the A♭ major, G♯ minor, A major, and A minor scales. The third pattern is started with the second finger. Simply through changing the starting position of the left hand, you can use this type of fingering to play all the remaining 18 scales. Therefore, as long as the three fingering patterns can be carefully studied first, it is not difficult to master all 24 three-octave scales.

To better learn the three fingering patterns, you can take the G major scale to study Fingering Pattern 1 first, then use the A major scale to study Fingering Pattern 2, and finally take the D major scale to study Fingering Pattern 3. (The three detailed fingerings for the arpeggios are also only shown in the G major, A major, and D major scales.) After the three fingerings are well mastered, you can use them to perform all 24 three-octave scales easily.

As some violinists do not like to start playing all 24 scales on the G string, in this book, an alternative fingering is provided to the scales which can be started on the D string. Therefore, one more fingering pattern is needed for these violinists. It is the fingering that always starts with the first finger on the D string. This type of fingering can be used to play the E♭ major, E♭ minor, E major, E minor, F major, F minor, F♯ major and F♯ minor 8 scales. (Please reference the fingering table 1B.) While studying, the E♭ major scale can be used to learn this type of fingering first. Then you can use this fingering to perform all other 7 scales simply through changing the starting position of the left hand on the D string.

Because the fingering classification for three-octave arpeggios and broken thirds is the same as for the scales, their fingering tables are not shown in this book. However, the three-octave chromatic scales have a very different character. Actually, the fingerings for three-octave chromatic scales are very simple. First, they all start with the first position of the left hand. Second, except a few lowest and highest notes, each absolute pitch always has its fixed fingering. So, it does not matter which scale you are going to play, the fingering difference among the scales only happens on the few lowest and highest notes. This fingering nature makes it much easier for violinist to master all 24 chromatic scales. While studying, you can take any one scale to learn the fingering first. Then, simply through the fingering changes on a few lowest and highest notes, you can perform all 24 chromatic scales easily.

Fingerings for Double-Stop Scales

It is more difficult to master all the double-stop scales because there are no unique fingering patterns available for all of them. In order to solve this problem, in this book, I first re-organize all the double-stop scales to make them simple, practical, and easy to learn. After re-organization, there are only six types of scales left. They are thirds, sixths, octaves, fingered octaves, tenths, and harmonic scales. These six scales can provide necessary exercises for violinists to build up their double-stop technique. Then I re-edit all their fingerings to make them as simple as possible. Let's take a look how it works.

Thirds: In this book, there are only two types of fingerings for thirds. The first one is the fingering that uses the 1st and 3rd fingers to play all the odd number notes of the scales. It usually begins with the 1st and 3rd fingers. Simply through changing the starting position of the left hand, you can use this type of fingering to play the A♭ major, G♯ minor, A major, A minor, C major, C minor, and C♯7 minor scales. The second type, on the contrary, uses the 2nd and 4th fingers to play all the odd number notes of the scales. It usually begins with at least one open string or both the 2nd and 4th fingers. All the remaining 17 scales, simply through changing the starting position of the left hand and the use of different strings, can be played with this type of fingering. Therefore, as long as you are clear what type of fingering is needed to play a specific scale, it is not difficult to master all 24 thirds scales. When practicing, you can take the A major scale to learn Fingering Pattern 1 first, and then take the D major scale to study Fingering Pattern 2. After the two fingerings are well mastered, you can use them to play all 24 thirds scales simply through changing the starting position of the left hand and the using of different strings.

Sixths: In this book, the fingerings for sixths are also very simple. First, though different scales start from different notes, when they reach the notes played by the 2nd and 3rd fingers on the A and E strings, these two fingers will be used to play all the remaining notes to reach the highest notes of the scale. After that, the same two fingers will be used to play all the descending notes back to the first position of the left hand. Then change the fingers to perform the remaining notes to finish the scale. Therefore, the fingering difference among all the sixths scales only happens between the beginning notes and the 2nd and 3rd fingers on the A and E strings. The fingerings for this part of the scales are usually straightforward. But some scales start and end at the 2nd or 3rd position of the left hand. The D♭ major, E♭ major, and E♭ minor scales start and end at the 2nd position. The A♭ major, G♯ minor, B♭ minor, and F minor scales start and end at the 3rd position. As long as these fingering changes are carefully studied, you should not have a problem performing all 24 sixths scales.

Fingered octaves: There are also only two types of fingerings for fingered-octave scales in this book. The first one is the fingering that uses the 2nd and 4th fingers to play all the odd number notes of the scales. It begins with one open string and the 2nd finger. This type of fingering is only used to play the G major, G minor, D major, and D minor scales, which start with one open string. The second one uses the 1st and 3rd fingers to play all the odd number notes of the scales. It begins with the 1st and 3rd fingers. All the remaining 20 scales, simply through changing the starting position of the left hand and the using of different strings, can be played by this type of fingering. (However, the fingerings for the descending part of the minor scales are different from major scales.) While practicing, you can take the G major and G minor scales to learn Fingering Pattern 1 first and then take the A major and A minor scales to study Fingering Pattern 2. After the two fingerings are well mastered, you can perform all 24 fingered-octave scales simply through changing the starting position of the left hand and the use of different strings.

Octaves, Tenths and Harmonic Scales: When performing octaves, tenths and harmonic scales, violinists almost have no choice for fingering. Basically, you just keep a nice hand frame with the 1st and 4th fingers to play the entire scale until the open strings are available. This fingering nature makes it easier for violinist to master all 24 scales. While performing octaves and tenths, it would be even better if you do not use open strings in the middle of the scales. By this way, the same fingering can be used to play many scales simply through changing the starting position of the left hand. In this book, both fingerings are listed. For those who want to play all 24 scales, the fingering without using open strings in the middle is recommended.

FINGERING PATTERNS FOR THREE-OCTAVE SCALES

(Table 1A)

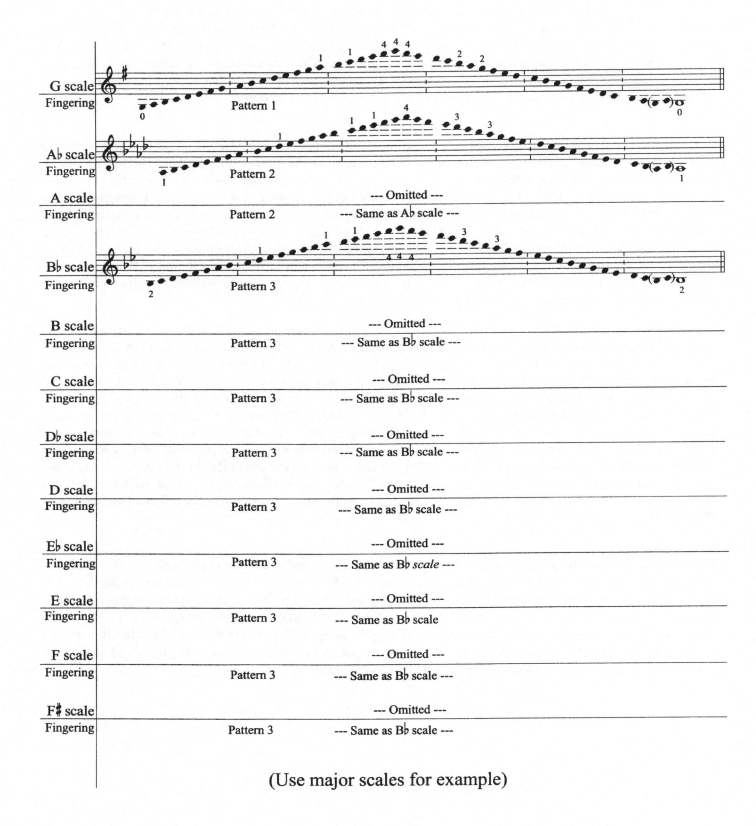

(Use major scales for example)

FINGERING PATTERNS FOR THREE-OCTAVE SCALES

(Table 1B)

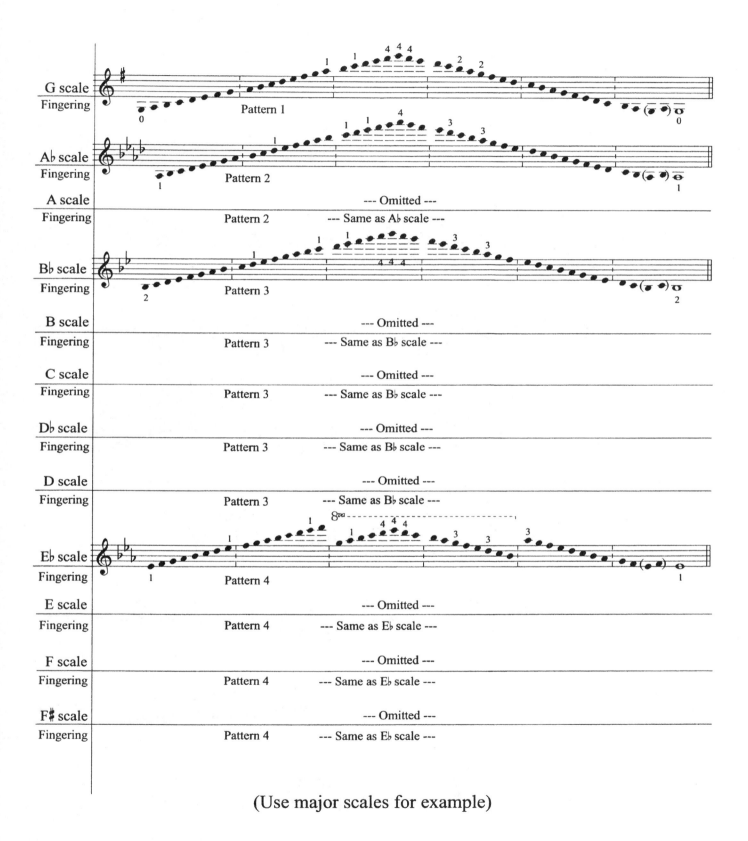

(Use major scales for example)

PART 1. DAILY SCALE EXERCISES
1. G major

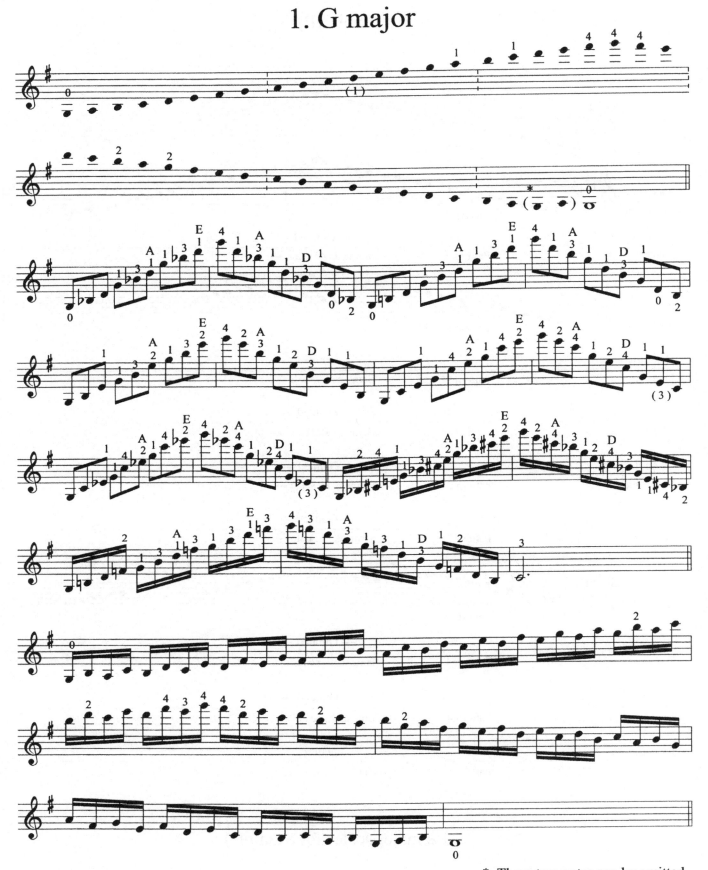

* These two notes can be omitted.

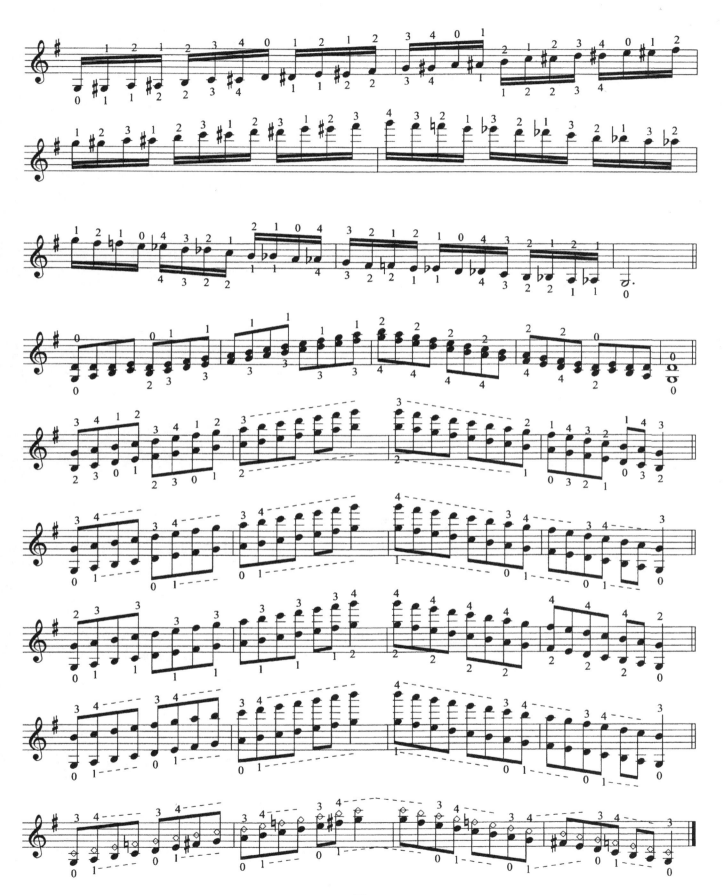

2. G minor

3. A♭ major

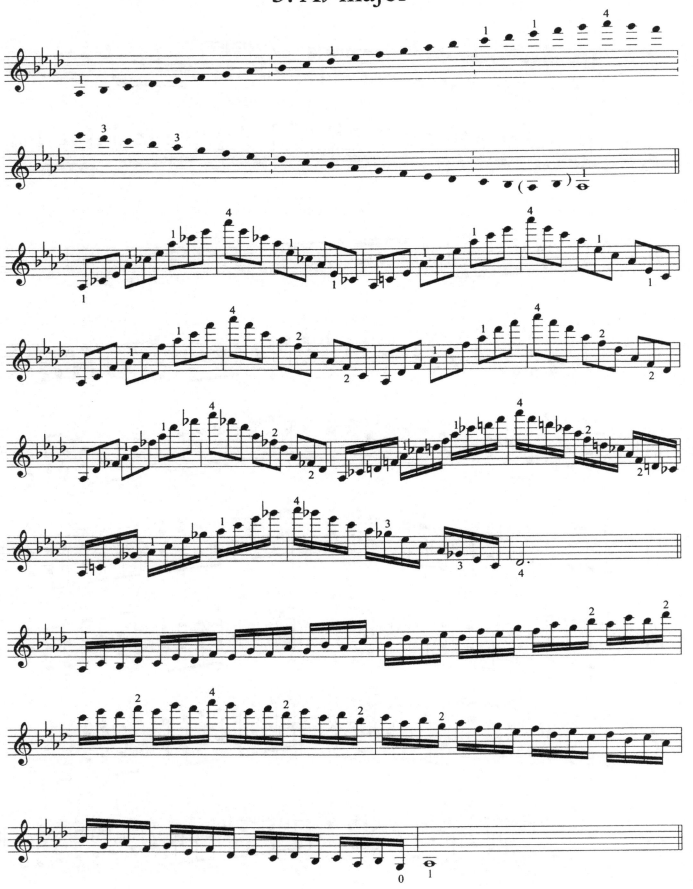

20

21

4. G♯ minor

23

5. A major

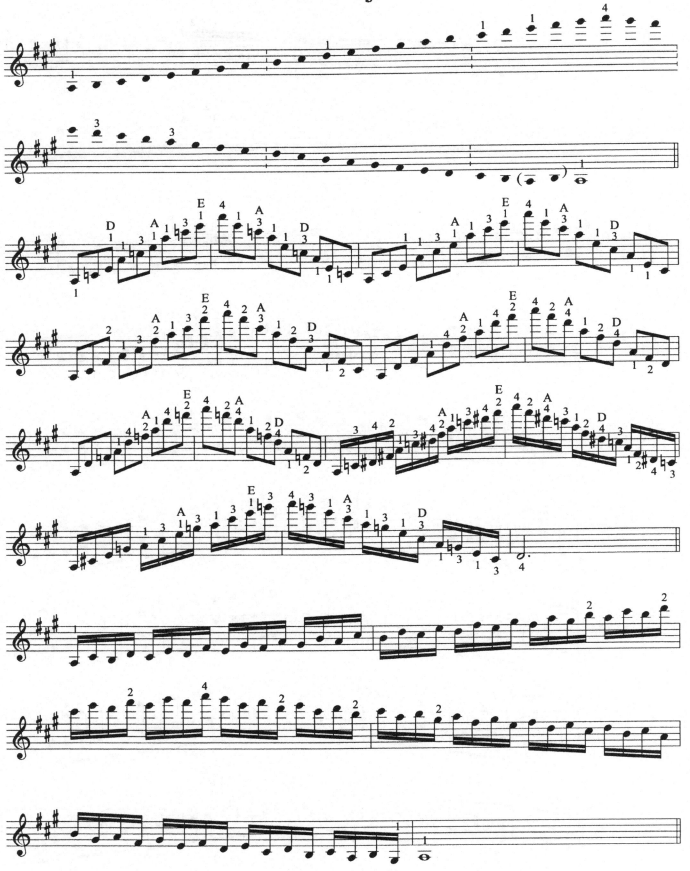

25

6. A minor

26

7. B♭ major

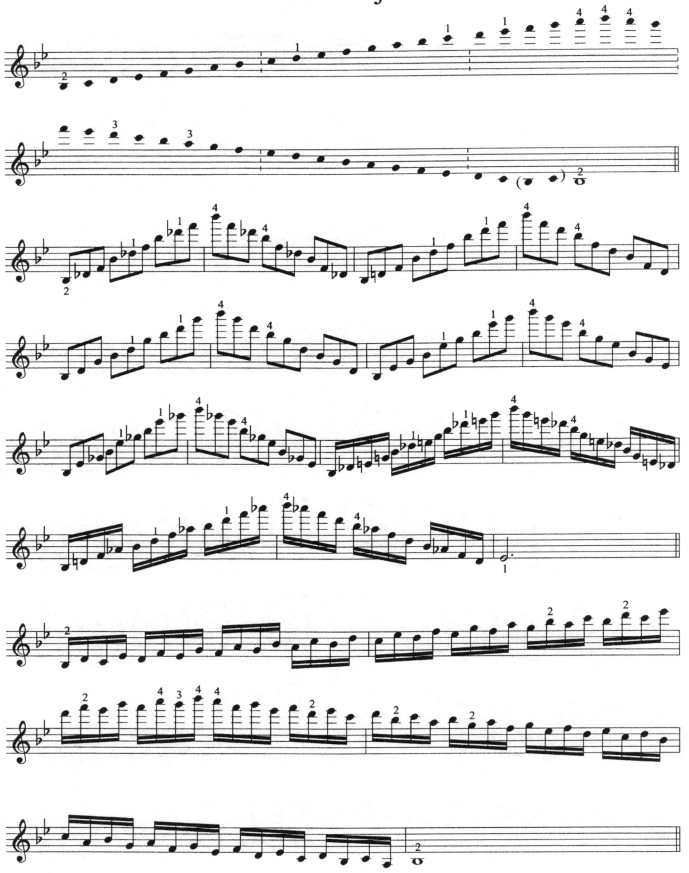

28

8. B♭ minor

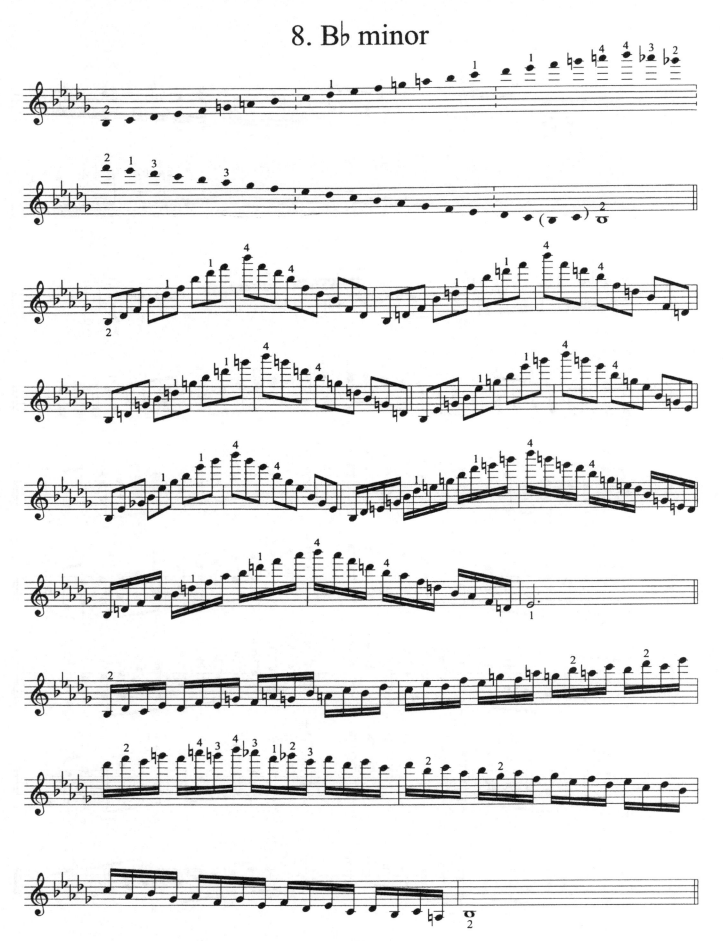

9. B major

33

10. B minor

11. C major

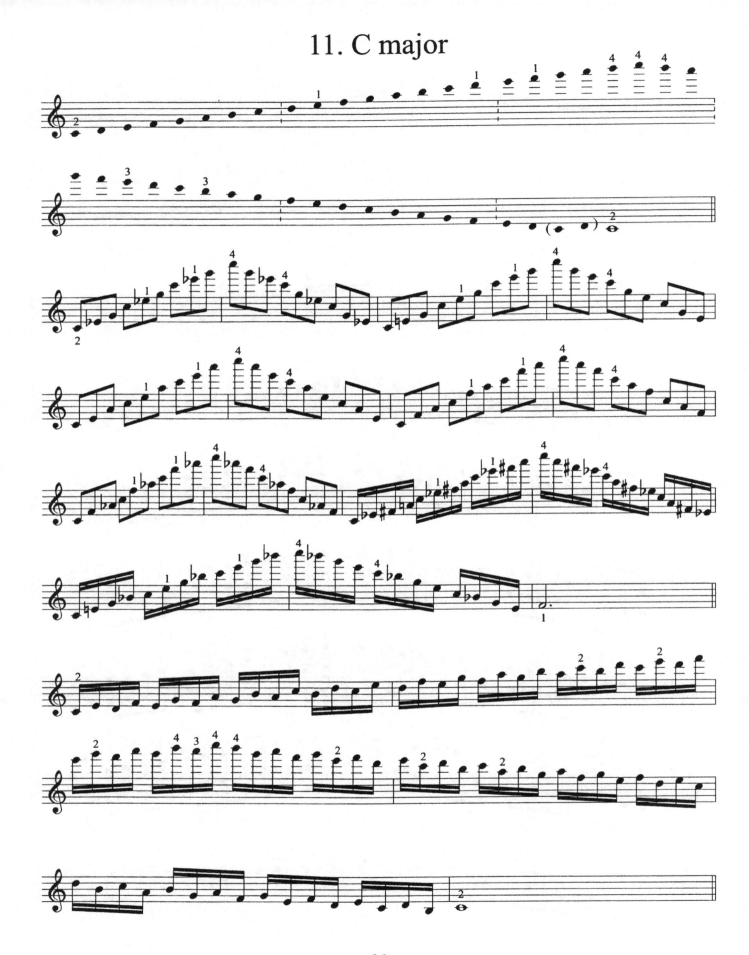

37

12. C minor

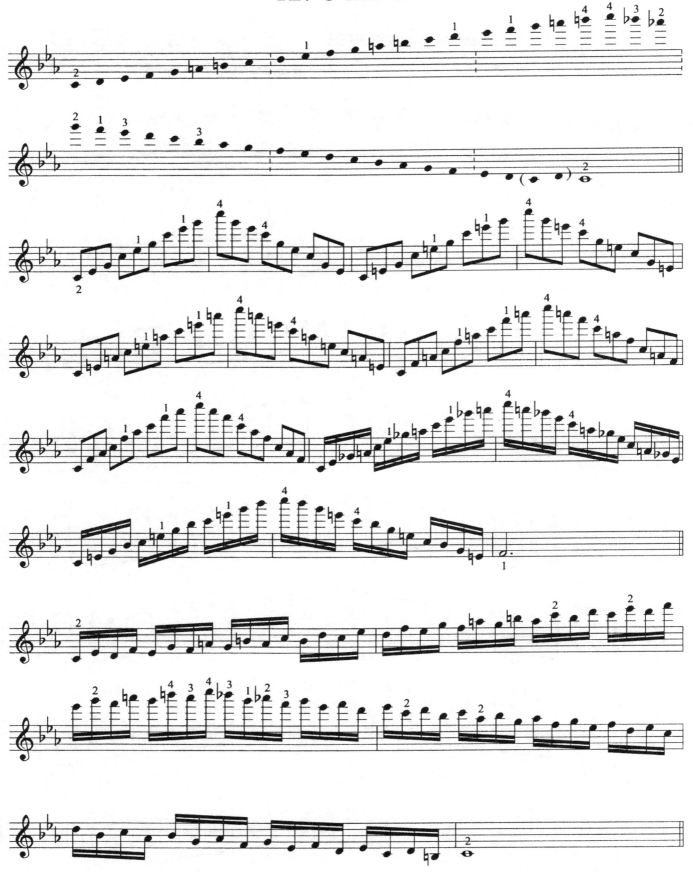

13. D♭ major

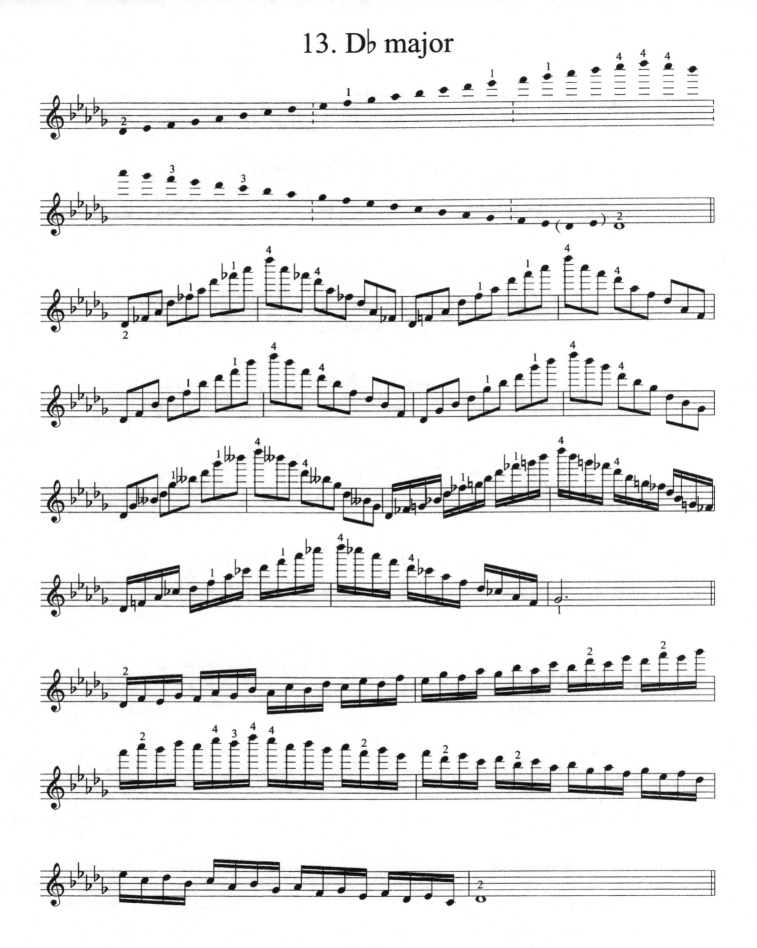

40

41

14. C# minor

15. D major

45

16. D minor

46

17. E♭ major

49

18. E♭ minor

50

51

19. E major

20. E minor

55

21. F major

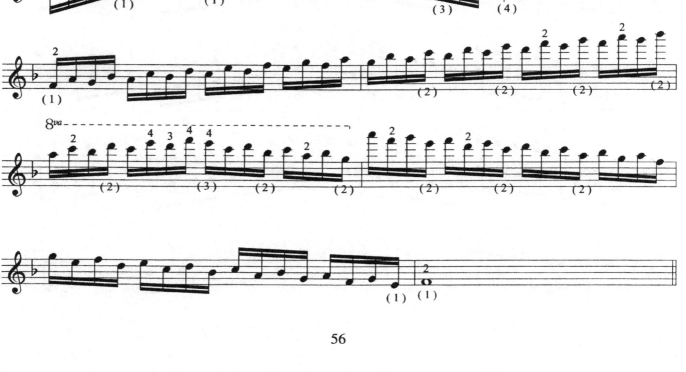

22. F minor

23. F♯ major

24. F♯ minor

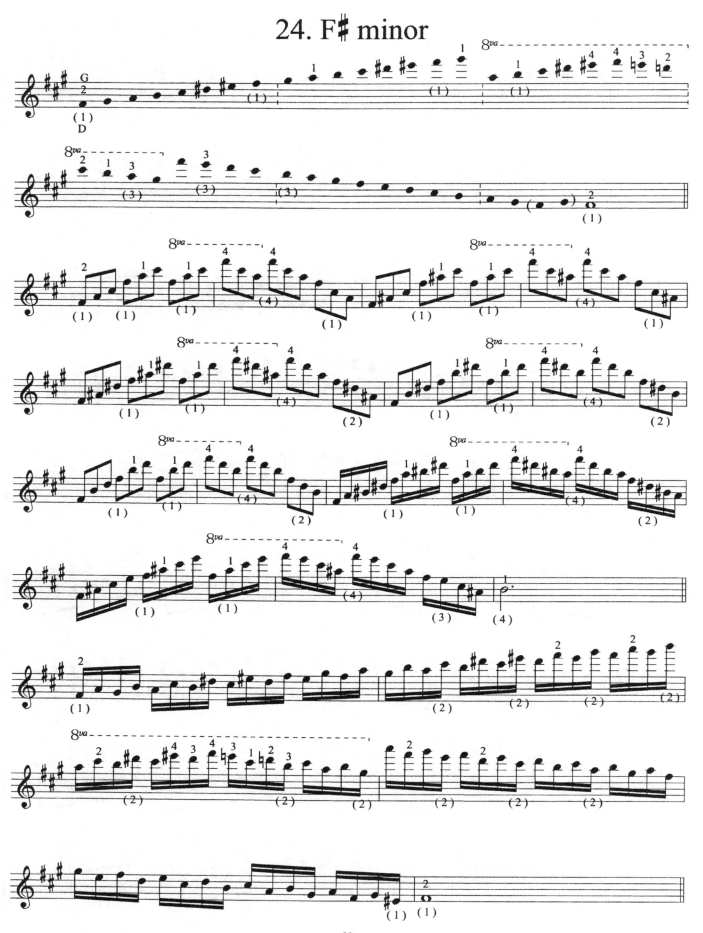

PART 2. FOUR-OCTAVE SCALES

Fingering Patterns for Four-Octave Scales

Four-octave scales are excellent exercises to promote left-hand technique. However, people usually do not pay attention to this type of exercises. So, I decided to add them into this book as a supplement to "DAILY SCALE EXERCISES". There are 6 of them in this book. All their fingerings can be classified into two patterns. The first one is the fingering started with the open string G. It is only used to play the G major and G minor scales. The second pattern is the fingering beginning with the first finger. It can be used to play the remaining 4 scales simply through changing the starting position of the left hand.

To better learn the two fingering patterns, you can take the G major scale to study the fingering pattern 1 first, and then use the A major scale to study the fingering pattern 2. When you have the two fingerings solidly in hand, you can use them to play all 6 four-octave scales easily.

There are no broken thirds and chromatic scales in the category of four-octave scales. As the fingering classification for the four-octave arpeggios is the same as for the scales, its' fingering table is not shown.

FINGERING PATTERNS FOR FOUR-OCTAVE SCALES

(Table 2)

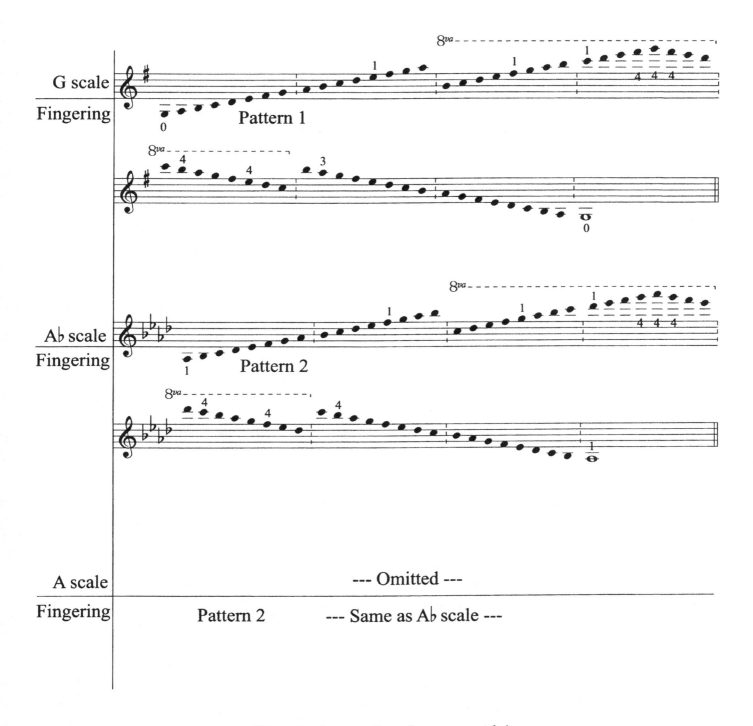

G scale	
Fingering	Pattern 1

Ab scale	
Fingering	Pattern 2

A scale	--- Omitted ---
Fingering	Pattern 2 --- Same as Ab scale ---

(Use major scales for example)

PART 2. FOUR-OCTAVE SCALES
25. G major

26. G minor

27. Ab major

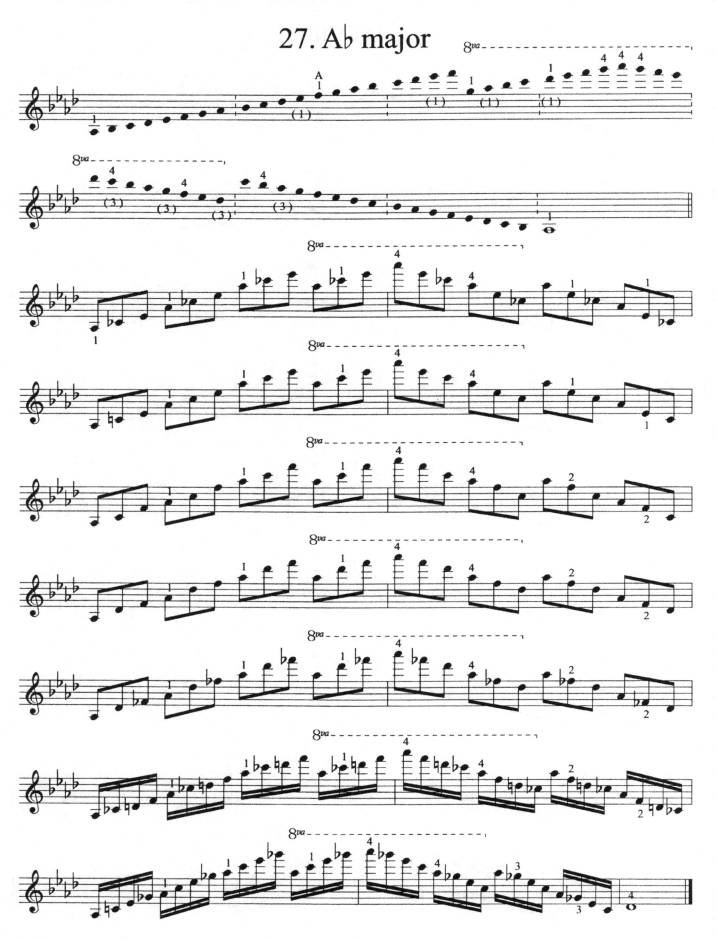

28. G♯ minor

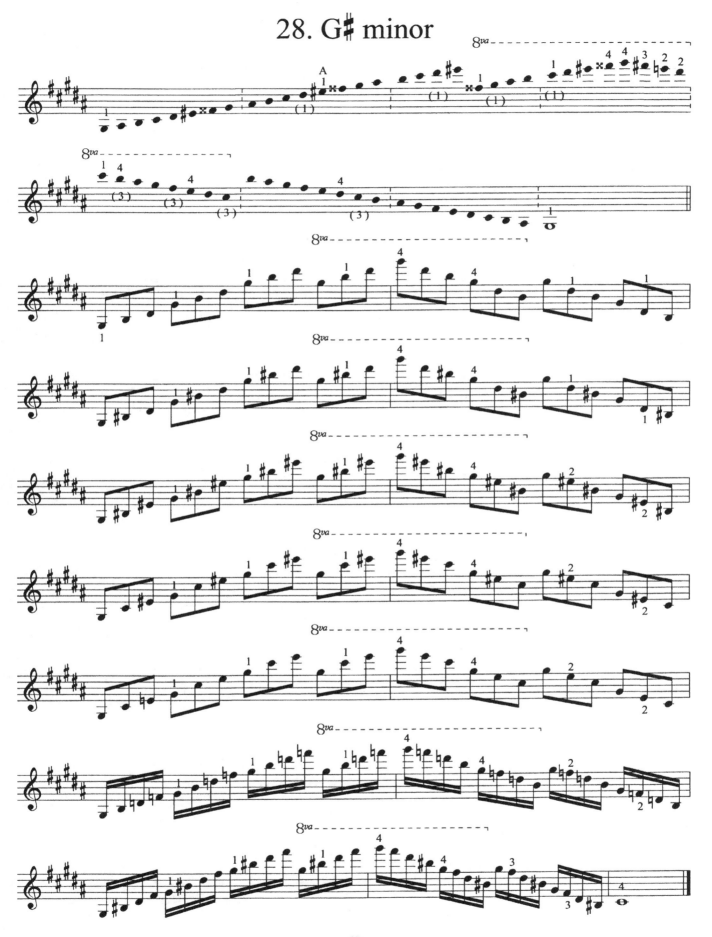

69

29. A major

70

30. A minor

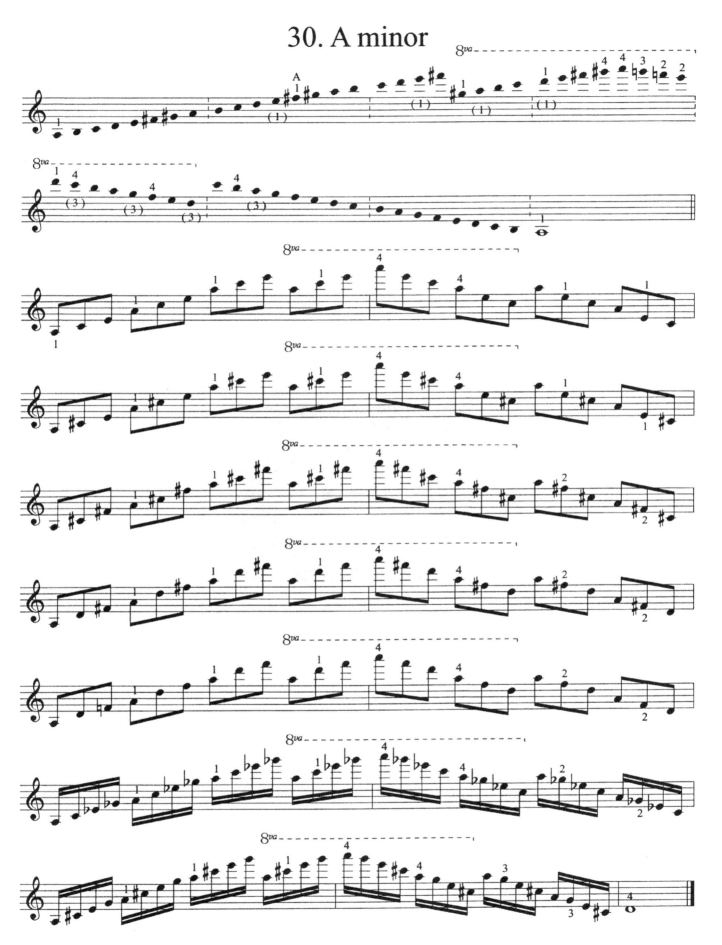